D1241463

# The Paint Box

Maxine Trottier • Stella East

Fitzhenry & Whiteside

Published in Canada by Fitzhenry & Whiteside,
195 Allstate Parkway, Markham, Ontario L3R 4T8

Published in the United States by Fitzhenry & Whiteside,
121 Harvard Avenue, Suite 2, Allston, Massachusetts 02134



www.fitzhenry.ca godwit@fitzhenry.ca

10 9 8 7 6 5 4 3 2 1

National Library of Canada Cataloguing in Publication

Trottier, Maxine
The paint box / Maxine Trottier, Stella East.

ISBN 1-55041-804-1 (bound).—ISBN 1-55041-808-4 (pbk.)

1. Tintoretto, Marietta, 1554-1590--Juvenile fiction. I. East, Stella II. Title.

PS8589.R685P34 2003 jC813'.54 C2002-905766-3
PZ7

U.S. Publisher Cataloging-in-Publication Data
(Library Congress Standards)

Trottier, Maxine.
The paint box / Maxine Trottier ; Stella East—1st ed.
[32] p. : col. ill. ; cm.
Summary: Marietta wants to paint like her father. But Marietta is a girl, and to work and study with her father she must disguise herself in boy's clothing.
IBSN 1-550471-804-1
ISBN 1-550471-808-4 (pbk.)
1. Artists — Fiction. 2. Renaissance — Italy — Fiction. I. East, Stella.
II. Title.
[E] 21 2003

Fitzhenry & Whiteside acknowledges with thanks the Canada Council for the Arts, the Government of Canada through the Book Publishing Industry Development Program (BPIDP), and the Ontario Arts Council for their support for our publishing program.

Printed in Hong Kong

For my father.
— M.T.

To Severin.
— S.E.

Long ago in Venice there was a girl named Marietta who loved to paint. She was the daughter of the great artist Tintoretto.

Her father adored her and took her everywhere, dressed in hose and a doublet, as a boy would be. The disguise was a secret held close between father and daughter. It gave Tintoretto the constant company of his dear child. It allowed Marietta the chance to learn, and to explore, the studios and galleries of Venice. For in those days, girls did not have such freedom.

Marietta was never without the paint box her father had given her. It was the color of a summer sky. Inside it she kept some of her paper and brushes, chalk, and sealed pots of paint. The box was her greatest treasure. Some day, Marietta knew, she would be an artist like her father.

"A gift from one painter to another, my dear," he said, when he gave her the paint box. "The work of an artist can fill the heart with light. Use it well, Marietta, and your heart will know happiness."

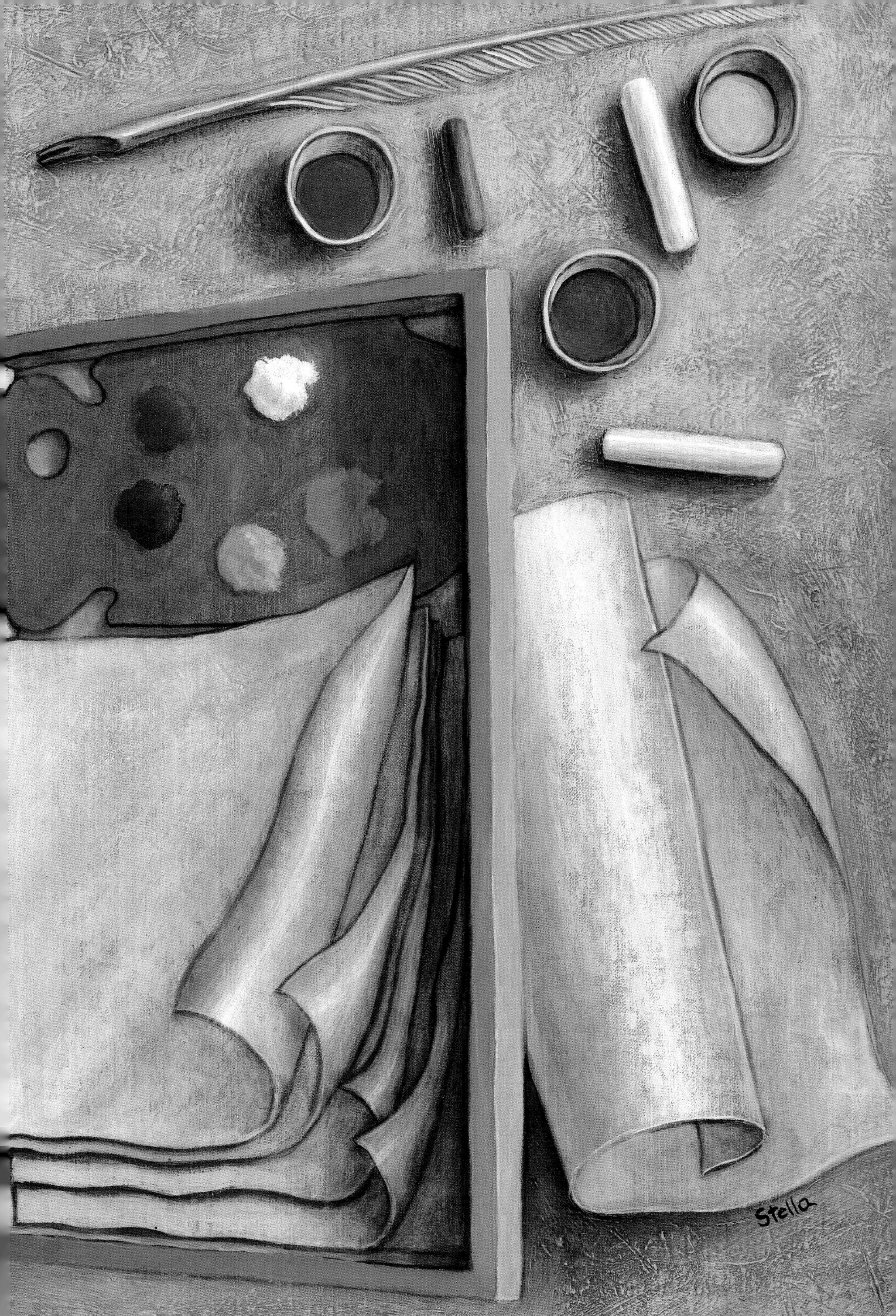
Stella

One midsummer's day, a wealthy sea captain came to Tintoretto's studio. The captain must have his portrait painted, it seemed. He posed, grand and mysterious, his gold earrings glittering. For a while, Marietta watched her father work. Then she looked outside.

A boy crouched below. He looked up and met her eyes. The smile he had for her was as warm as the sun.

"I must draw him!" Marietta cried. Her father laughed and nodded as he turned back to his painting. He could deny her nothing.

The captain glanced down through the window. He did not see anything special, only the slave who was his cabin boy. "What use is a cabin boy without a ship?" he said. "He is yours for as long as I am here."

Down the stairs Marietta hurried, her paint box in her hands. There was the boy, kneeling and sketching on the stones with a bit of charcoal.

"For a coin I would draw your face, my lord," he offered.

"I would much rather draw yours," answered Marietta. "And I am no lord at all!"

The lad's eyes grew wide and then he laughed. "What a clever disguise!"

"It is a fact of my life," Marietta sighed. "I cannot wander Venice dressed in a gown if I am to study as I must. I am as bound to these clothes as you are to your master."

The boy's name was Piero, and he was indeed owned by the captain. Piero told Marietta how he had been sold so that his brothers and sisters would have bread to eat. They had stood in a silent line when Piero was led away, the tears dripping down their faces. But his grandfather — his grandfather had wept aloud that day.

Stella

Marietta and Piero were as different as the sun and the moon, and yet somehow, they were the same. It was their love of drawing that made it so. For the days that followed they were inseparable.

On clear mornings they might walk through the city looking for something new to sketch. Or Marietta might watch Piero draw his grandfather's face on the stones.

Sometimes they took out Marietta's small boat. They made their way up and down the canals, passing stately gondolas that floated by like black swans. Tired and sunburned at the end of a long day, they would tie the little vessel in the canal behind the studio. On rainy afternoons they sat together, heedless of the weather, dangling their feet in the water, watching raindrops make a thousand rings upon its green surface.

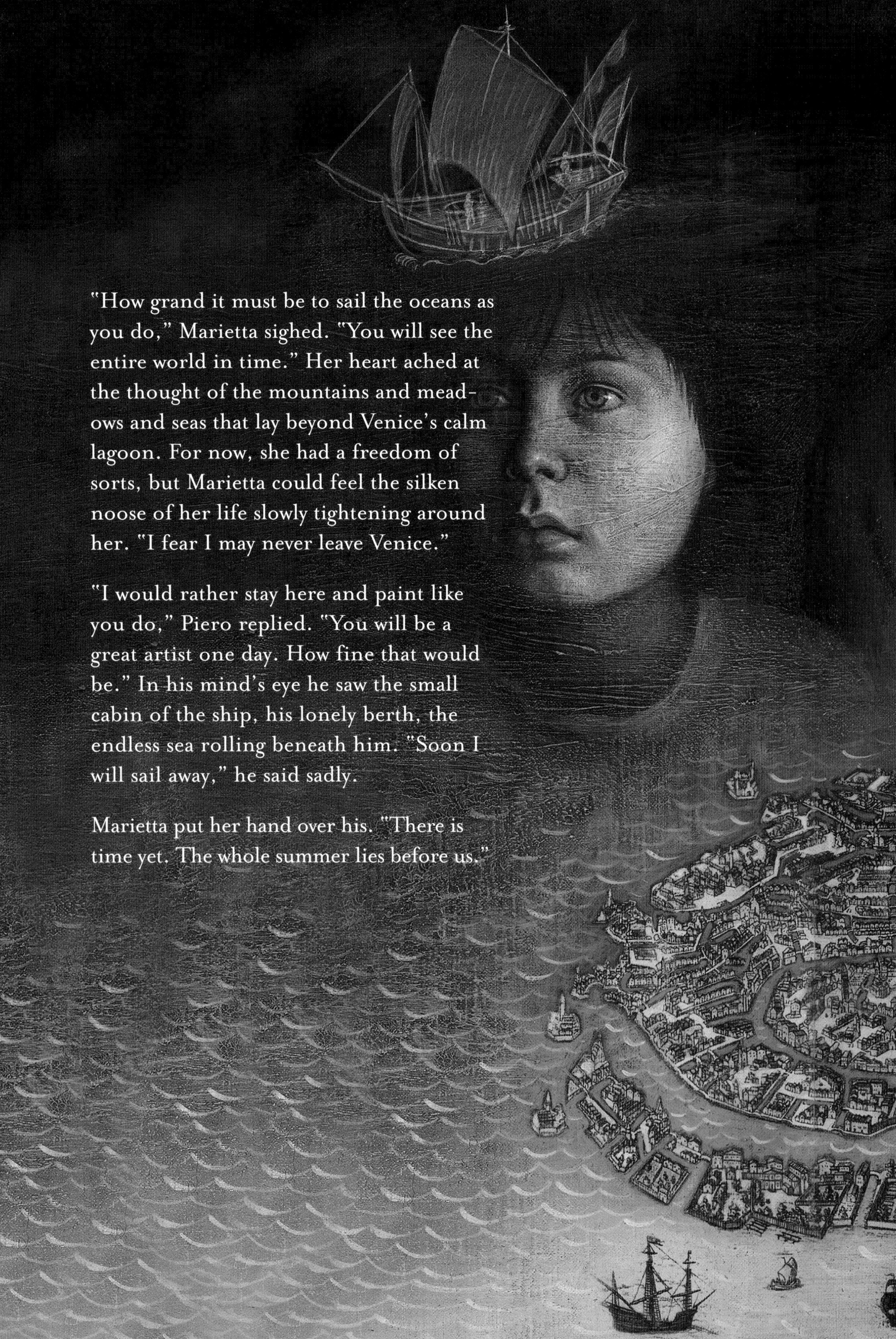

"How grand it must be to sail the oceans as you do," Marietta sighed. "You will see the entire world in time." Her heart ached at the thought of the mountains and meadows and seas that lay beyond Venice's calm lagoon. For now, she had a freedom of sorts, but Marietta could feel the silken noose of her life slowly tightening around her. "I fear I may never leave Venice."

"I would rather stay here and paint like you do," Piero replied. "You will be a great artist one day. How fine that would be." In his mind's eye he saw the small cabin of the ship, his lonely berth, the endless sea rolling beneath him. "Soon I will sail away," he said sadly.

Marietta put her hand over his. "There is time yet. The whole summer lies before us."

Stella

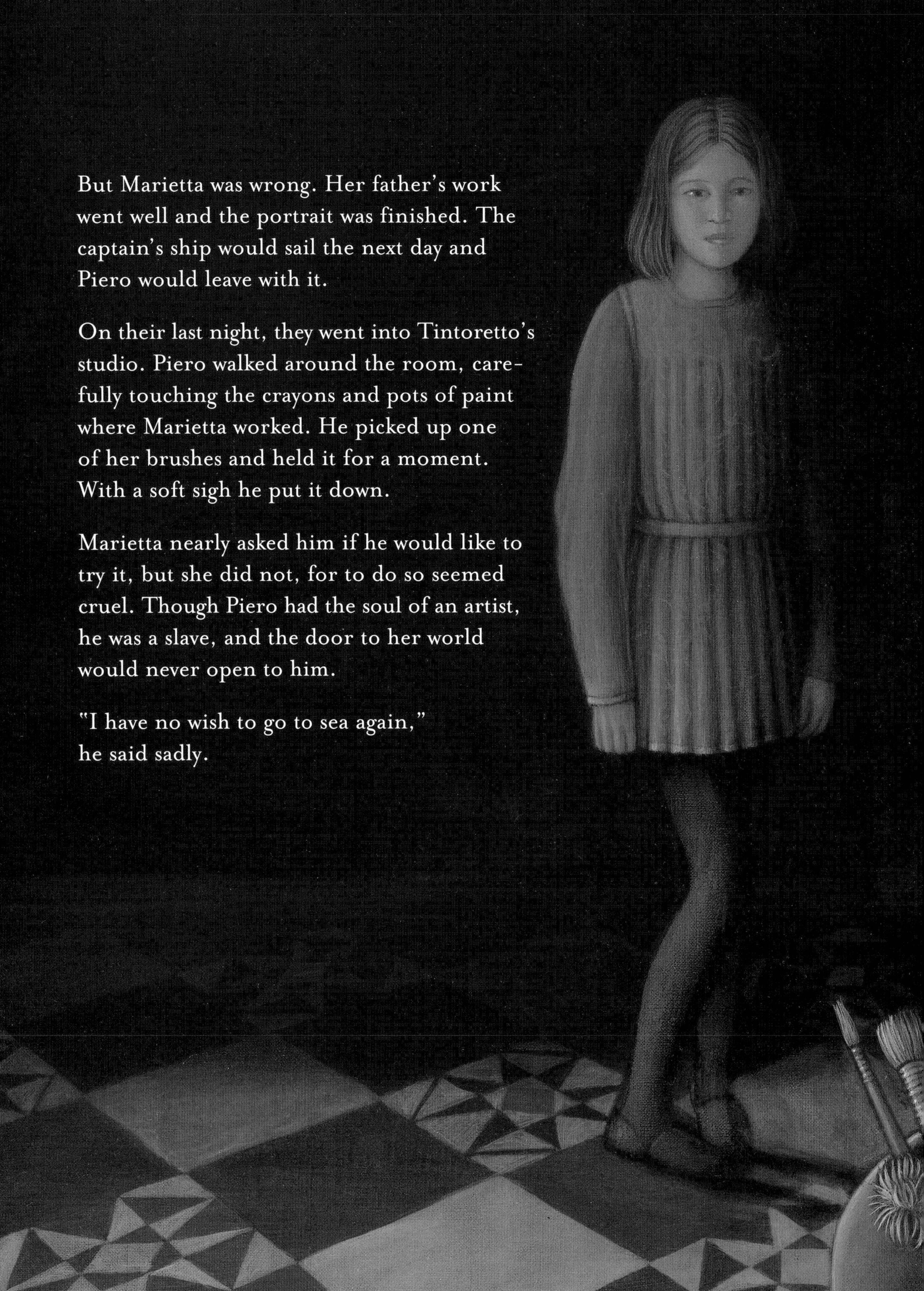

But Marietta was wrong. Her father's work went well and the portrait was finished. The captain's ship would sail the next day and Piero would leave with it.

On their last night, they went into Tintoretto's studio. Piero walked around the room, carefully touching the crayons and pots of paint where Marietta worked. He picked up one of her brushes and held it for a moment. With a soft sigh he put it down.

Marietta nearly asked him if he would like to try it, but she did not, for to do so seemed cruel. Though Piero had the soul of an artist, he was a slave, and the door to her world would never open to him.

"I have no wish to go to sea again," he said sadly.

Stella

Without a word, Marietta took up her paint box and led Piero from the studio. They walked across the darkening courtyard toward the archway that led to the canal. "No one will look for you here," she told him firmly. "After the captain has sailed, take my boat and set out on your own. You can return to your grandfather."

In the gloom of the archway, Marietta stopped. She looked down at her paint box and stroked its lid. There are different kinds of slavery, she thought. I am bound to one thing and he to another. Thinking of her father and how dearly he loved her, she held the box out to Piero. "From one artist to another," she whispered.

"I have nothing to give you," Piero said helplessly.

"To know you are free will be enough." Marietta turned to look at him one last time before she left. They smiled at each other, and then she was gone.

Piero opened the paint box and stared at the fine chalks and charcoals. He did not go to sleep for many hours, but when at last he stepped into Marietta's boat, he was weary and very happy. Like a little bird in its nest, he was rocked to sleep.

Stella

They called and searched for him the next morning, but Piero could not be found. In the end, the captain took his finished portrait and set sail. Marietta knew Piero was safe.

Stella

Late that afternoon, Marietta walked to the place where her boat had always been tied. It would be gone. She did not have to look to know. Still, she continued under the archway toward the canal.

Marietta stopped, her eyes wide. The walls were covered with drawings. Piero had sketched mountains wreathed in mist, valleys deep and green. Sleepy farms drowsed under the sun and silent monasteries stood watchful and still. An ocean lay in the distance, and on it floated a small boat with two young people in it. One was Piero. The other was Marietta.

Marietta never saw Piero again. In time his drawings would slowly fade, growing dimmer and dimmer, until they were like ghosts who had once lived and loved and breathed. But for today, they were very alive. Marietta closed the door upon the pictures, and with a heart filled with light, went to her father's studio to paint.



Stella

# Author's Note

With permission: Kunsthistorisches Museum, Wien oder KHM, Wien

Marietta Tintoretto was the daughter of Jacopo Tintoretto, a renowned Venetian artist. She was born in 1560 during the Renaissance. In Venice, it was a time when the arts were truly celebrated; a period of awakening and freedom and fresh ideas. But Marietta was a girl. To work and study with her father, he had her dress in boy's clothing so that she might accompany him wherever he went. She became a very talented artist. In spite of the fact that she was invited to be a court painter, Marietta never left Venice. She married and later died in childbirth at the age of thirty-four.

For a long while it was believed that Marietta had simply been her father's assistant. In 1920, however, the painting *Portrait of an Old Man with Boy* was attributed to her. Marietta's signature, a small *m*, had been discovered on its surface.

Some scholars think that the old man in the work was Marietta's grandfather, Marco dei Vescovi. On the other hand, it is possible that like the fictional Piero and his grandfather, the two people came into Marietta's world briefly, then simply disappeared again. Whoever they were, the old man and the boy live on in this painting. That a story or image still stirs the heart after its creator is gone, is a wonderful tribute.

My thanks to two artists: Marietta Patricia Leis, whose own work was so helpful in the writing of this story, and Stella East, who inspired it, and whose paintings brought it to life.